Copyright © 1984 Original Appalachian Artworks, Inc. Published in the United States by Parker Brothers, Division of CPG Products Corp. Cabbage Patch Kids™ and the character names contained in this book are trademarks of and licensed from Original Appalachian Artworks, Inc. Cleveland, GA. U.S.A. All rights reserved.

Library of Congress Cataloging in Publication Data: Xavier's fantastic discovery. (Cabbage Patch kids).
SUMMARY: Xavier Roberts follows a Bunny Bee through a waterfall and, after finding himself in a magical land where children grow in cabbage patches, helps to save two of the children from kidnappers.
[1. Kidnapping—Fiction] I. McQueen, Lucinda, ill. II. Title. III. Series
PZ7.S3466Fan 1984 [E] 83-20446 ISBN 0-910313-25-3
Manufactured in the United States of America 1 2 3 4 5 6 7 8 9 0

Xavier's
Fantastic Discovery

Pictures by Lucinda McQueen

Special thanks to Roger and Susanne Schlaifer
for bringing the legend to life.

Xavier was ten that summer — well, he'd probably say ten and three-quarters — and since school was out for the summer, he was visiting his Aunt Patty and Uncle John. Aunt Patty was his daddy's sister, and she and Uncle John had taken a special interest in Xavier's upbringing since his daddy died.

Aunt Patty and Uncle John lived near Mt. Yonah where the Georgia mountains start coming down to earth before becoming forest, hills, and flatlands. Farther to the south was the great swamp.

Aunt Patty and Uncle John were fine folks, but they didn't have any children of their own for Xavier to play with. And they didn't have any neighbors who did, either.

So Xavier spent the quiet hours dreaming of magical things and drawing pictures of all he dreamed about. Sometimes, when Uncle John wasn't too busy on the farm, he would take Xavier fishing, exploring, or camping. And that's how Xavier came to know the mountains, woods, and creeks that stretched out for miles around the farm.

Now, on this particular day, Xavier was feeling all grown-up because for the first time ever, he was being allowed to go camping all by himself. He was backpacking in the mountains, whistling a tune he'd just made up and halfway looking for some place alongside the river to make camp, when — all of a sudden — he heard a buzzing kind of noise. He looked about for a minute and finally saw what seemed to be making the sound: a sort of good-sized bee, but different. And as it got closer, Xavier saw on its head, working like wings, what for all the world looked like the ears of a tiny rabbit. Suddenly, the thing did a loop-de-loop and headed off in the other direction.

"What in tarnation!" said Xavier as he saw its going-away view, bit of white fluff where a bunny tail would have been if this had been a bunny instead of . . . whatever it was.

Then off it flew toward a dense stand of pine a little upstream. Xavier decided he'd follow for a while and see if the "bee-bunny" or "bunny-bee" lived in a burrow like a bunny or in a hive like a bee. And whether it would nibble grass or look for the pollen in a flower. So he set about following it along the edge of the woods, where the BunnyBee just meandered through the air above the bushes and among the trees. Then Xavier heard a commotion in the underbrush.

Since he didn't know just what was in there, Xavier reached down and picked up a hefty stick before he edged closer. All the while, the BunnyBee waited to see what would happen. Suddenly, a huge head poked out from the bushes.
It seemed to be looking up in the air for something, maybe the BunnyBee, but it saw Xavier instead. And Xavier saw *it!*

Now there was no mistaking what it was. It was the biggest rabbit that Xavier had ever seen, bar none. And the worst part was that he saw right off that it wasn't just big, it was *mean!* As it looked him square in the eye, it bared its teeth, which sure didn't look like regular rabbit teeth, and made a rumbling growl that a normal rabbit would never have dreamed of.

Xavier was more than a little scared, but this being a day when he was feeling grown-up, he raised his stick at that big rabbit and began making faces and hollering, "Woogie-woogie!" at the top of his lungs. If the rabbit was scared, Xavier couldn't tell. It just stared at Xavier for a minute, then turned and went back into the underbrush.

As Xavier listened to the heavy clomp of the jackrabbit's feet, he started having second thoughts about camping out in the woods that night. If rabbits grew that big and mean around there, what would the other creatures be like? He started looking for the BunnyBee again, and soon he saw it.

The BunnyBee was flying along the riverbank in the direction of Mount Yonah, and as it got farther away Xavier relied on its sound to keep track of it. Soon something started to drown out the strange buzz that the BunnyBee made. It was the sound of a waterfall; and as Xavier hurried along, the sound got louder.

Just ahead of him, he saw the BunnyBee hovering in midair. Maybe it was deciding where to head next, and maybe it was just waiting for Xavier to catch up. Xavier could see the clear water cascading off the mountain, but before he could catch up, the BunnyBee flew straight into the waterfall and disappeared.

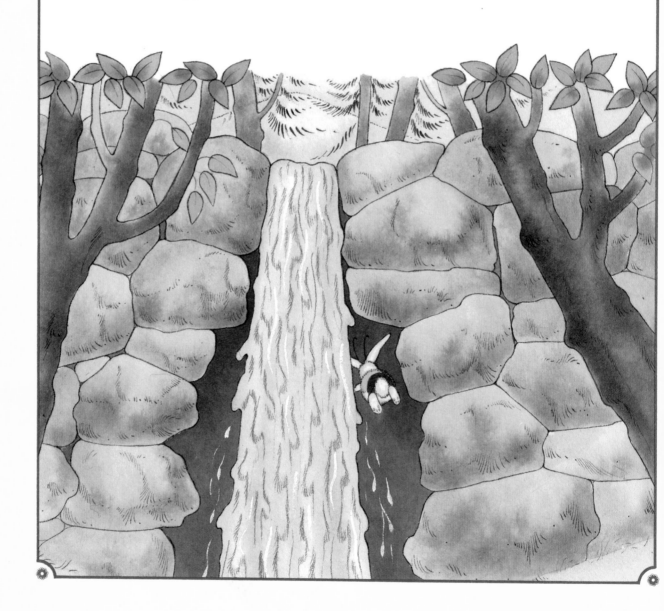

"Poor, bitty thing. You're drowned for sure," Xavier exclaimed.

Now, anybody but Xavier Roberts might have thought all this was pretty unlikely, but Xavier had a keen imagination. He was always thinking up strange adventures, and this was beginning to seem like a good one! Xavier scrambled down the red, clay bank and over some rocks next to the waterfall where the BunnyBee had disappeared. And soon he discovered where the BunnyBee had gone.

Getting down on his hands and knees, he crawled through a small space between the water and rocks and found himself in a cave. The floor was flat and the ceiling high. And here and there great rainbow spirals rose up from the floor and hung down from the ceiling. As Xavier got deeper into the cave, the light became more and more dim. He stopped to pull out his flashlight, all the time hoping the cave didn't have bats and other scary things like the ones he'd seen in the movies.

As he went along in the dark, every kind of scary creature he'd ever imagined (including that giant rabbit which he *hadn't* imagined) seemed to be peering at him from hidden spaces in the cave.

But a voice kept running through his head, saying, "There's adventure ahead . . . there's adventure ahead." And he remembered his daddy's funny way of scaring off the night creatures that sometimes sneaked into his room at bedtime when he was real little. "What night creatures hate the most," his daddy would say, "is a good joke. And if you can't think of a good joke right away, just make the funniest face you can, and say 'Woogie-woogie.'" Well, it always seemed to work when he was little, and after all, it *did* work with that rabbit.

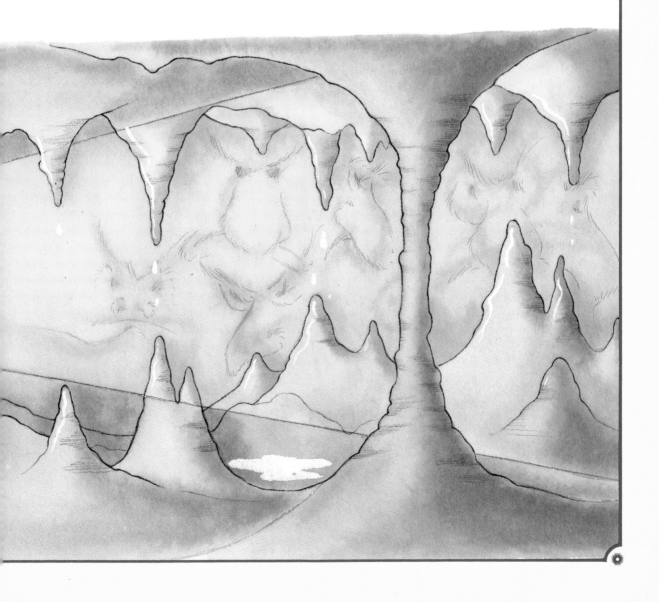

So Xavier screwed up his face into the weirdest look he could, and started saying, "Woogie-woogie." At first it sort of stuck in his throat, his heart having jammed up somewhere in that general vicinity. But soon he was "Woogie-woogie-ing" his way through the cave, almost making it into a song.

After what seemed to be a long time in the blackness of the cave, Xavier saw what he thought were little specks of light up ahead, and he headed straight toward them. Before long, he found himself face to face with a thick wall of kudzu vine.

Sure enough, there was daylight peeking through the kudzu. Putting down his flashlight, Xavier pulled out his trusty scout knife and started cutting through the snarled and twisted vines. It didn't take him long to cut an opening in the kudzu large enough to walk through. Stepping out of the darkness of the cave, he blinked his eyes a few times to adjust to the bright sunlight.

Xavier suddenly found himself in a beautiful valley, separated on all sides from the mountains he knew so well by walls of kudzu. Inside he saw rows and rows of cabbages. BunnyBees like the one Xavier had followed were flying above the cabbages. As they buzzed around, they swooped gracefully and left trails of sparkling crystals, which floated down onto the cabbages. Or rather, all swooped gracefully except one BunnyBee who was wearing a helmet; he kept bumping into the others and falling into the flowers. Xavier later discovered that this was the Stumble-Bumble BunnyBee.

A rope swing was hanging from one of the oaks, swaying as if someone had just left it. Xavier had at first heard a hum of activity, but it had stopped. Except for the buzz of the Bunnybees, an unnatural silence hung in the air.

Remembering that he had left his flashlight just inside the cave, Xavier turned around to reach for it. To his surprise, he saw that the vines had already grown back to cover the cave opening completely. "That's strange," Xavier said aloud, "I never knew kudzu could grow so fast."

"Everything grows fast in the Cabbage Patch," said a voice.

Xavier nearly jumped out of his skin at that. "Who said that? Who's there?" he demanded.

There was a slight rustling in the cabbage leaves before two little boys stepped shyly out into the open.

Xavier wasn't sure what he was seeing. These boys didn't look like any other kids he had seen before.

"Pleased to meet you," said the first one. "My name is Otis Lee, and this is my pal, Tyler Bo." With that, the boys reached out to shake hands with Xavier.

"Hi, my name's Xavier Roberts, and I'm pleased to meet you, too."

"We didn't mean to be hiding from you, but we were a little startled when you popped out of our secret cave like that," explained Otis Lee.

"Yeah, we were afraid maybe that oversized, mangey rabbit called Cabbage Jack had finally figured out how to sneak into the Cabbage Patch," added Tyler Bo.

Xavier remembered the rabbit he had encountered back in the woods. "This Cabbage Jack, is he big, with teeth that . . ."

"That's him," confirmed Otis.

Xavier looked puzzled, "But why would he be trying to sneak into your Cabbage Patch? I always thought rabbits preferred carrots to cabbages."

"Oh, it's not the cabbages he's after," said Otis Lee shaking his head, "it's us 'Kids."

"'Kids?"

"Right, Cabbage Patch Kids." Taking Xavier by the hand, Otis led him over to the cabbages. "You see, here's where we come from. The BunnyBees' magic crystals make the cabbages grow into 'Kids like us. Then Colonel Casey..."

Just then a large shadow loomed in their path, and an old stork landed with a swoosh.

"Mornin', Colonel Casey. Tyler and I were just telling Xavier..."

Colonel Casey eyed Xavier suspiciously. "Well, young man, would you care to explain to me who you might be and just how you managed to get here?"

"Yes sir, my name is Xavier Roberts, and I was out backpacking along the river when I saw this BunnyBee..."

"Hmmph. Otis, are you boys sure about this?"

"Oh, yes sir, Colonel Casey, he's going to be our friend."

"Really, he is," added Tyler Bo.

"Well, if you say so; you 'Kids seem to have a knack for telling the good from the bad. But where are all the other 'Kids?"

"Oops!" said Otis, "We got so carried away explaining things to Xavier, we forgot to tell them the coast is clear. It's okay," Otis yelled. "He's a friend."

Soon, 'Kids were coming from everywhere – from behind bushes and trees and from under the cabbage leaves – all looking at Xavier and wondering what was going on. A few of the braver ones edged up closer to get a better look.

One little girl named Sybil Sadie, who was not as shy as some of the others, pushed her way into the middle of things, put her hands on her hips, and started asking questions.

"All right, Otis, who is this?"

"Xavier Roberts, a person. Xavier, meet Sybil Sadie."

Xavier was grinning from ear to ear, "Hi, Sybil Sadie."

But Sybil Sadie wasn't quite ready to be friends. "How did you get here?" she demanded.

Before Xavier could answer, Tyler Bo gave Sybil Sadie a reproachful look and said, "Don't be so snippy. He's okay."

Otis continued to introduce Xavier to the other 'Kids. "And this is Rachel Marie — Ramie for short — and Marilyn Suzanne. And this is Baby Dodd."

Baby Dodd looked up at Xavier and reached out his arms, "Wo," he said.

"He's still pretty young," said Ramie. " 'Wo' is his way of saying hello."

Xavier blushed, "I . . . I'm afraid I don't know much about babies."

"Well," said Colonel Casey, "you'll sure learn fast 'round here. Come on. I've got a delivery out here who's beginnin' to sound mighty impatient."

Following Colonel Casey, Xavier was amazed to find a baby nestled in the cabbage leaves who was sort of crying and cooing all at the same time. Bending over, the Colonel slid a blanket underneath the baby and scooped him up.

"My next job is to find a place to put this young'un. I don't suppose you've had time to notice, but his valley is just about plum filled up. What with delivering babies 'round the clock and trying to keep the 'Kids out of the way of Lavendar McDade and her sleazy gang, I just haven't had the time to scout for new homes for all the 'Kids. I'm not as young as I used to be, you know. Why don't we rest a spell and I'll tell you all about the Cabbage Patch."

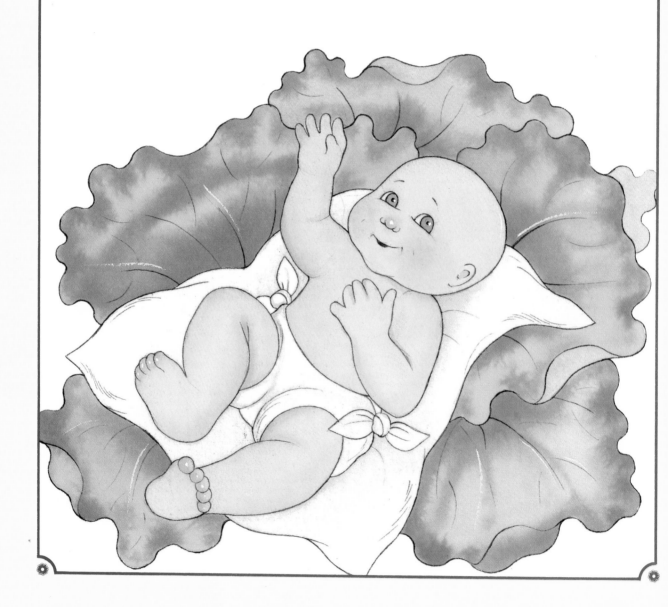

"First off," said Colonel Casey, "I'd better fill you in on Lavendar McDade and what she's up to. Lavendar is a greedy old woman who lives south of here. She's as mean as a snake. It seems there's an old gold mine near her place, and she's trying to get it going again. The way she sees it, there's no need in paying anybody to work the mine when there's plenty of Cabbage Patch Kids around just for the taking. The worst part is, she's not in this alone. She's got Cabbage Jack helpin' her. Sometimes she brings in others, too. Now that she's set eyes on that gold, there's no tellin' what kind of varmits will be creepin' about."

"How do you protect yourselves?" Xavier asked.

"Lavendar hasn't found out where the Cabbage Patch is yet. 'Course the 'Kids can't seem to stay in the 'Patch all the time — always wantin' to go off and look for adventure — but we've got a few tricks up our sleeves. And of course there are the BB-Bees . . ."

While Colonel Casey was telling Xavier about the BB-Bees and some of the Cabbage Patch Kids' other friends, Lavendar McDade was in the basement of her house trying to think of ways to capture 'Kids. She was in a frightful temper.

"I've got all that gold down there, but the shaft in that part of the mine is too narrow for us to get into." Turning to glare at Cabbage Jack, Lavendar demanded, "Where are those 'Kids you promised?"

"Well, I was following the BunnyBee with the magic crystals, when all of a sudden there was this boy with a big stick, and . . ."

"Excuses! That's all I get from you! What kind of evil rabbit are you, anyway? For all the good you're doing me, you might as well be the Easter Bunny. I'm tired of waiting, you oversized rodent! I've brought in a specialist from the swamp. His name is Beau Weasel, and I hope he can get some results out of you."

Upon hearing his name, Beau Weasel slunk into the room. "Greetings, friends. I hope I'll be able to assist you in your stupendously sly schemes."

Cabbage Jack looked anything but happy. "What am *I* supposed to do now that he's here?"

"You'll work *with* him, that's what you'll do," snapped Lavendar.

Beau Weasel walked over and put his arm around Cabbage Jack. "Patience, C.J., there's enough gold in that mine for all of us."

"You two cut out the pleasantries and get on with what I'm paying you for," said Lavendar.

While Lavendar McDade and her gang were plotting, Baby Dodd had wandered out of the 'Patch. Now, the 'Kids were calling his name as they searched for him.

Ramie looked worried. "He must have slipped out of the 'Patch while we weren't looking," she said.

Gilda Mae started wringing her hands. "He's probably gone to eat some more blackberries. Colonel Casey and Otis are going to skin us for letting him out of our sight."

Not being one to waste time worrying, Sybil Sadie started giving orders. "We'll just have to go and find him right away. Marilyn Suzanne, you come with me."

"I'm not going out there and rooting around in those blackberries. I'd ruin my dress," complained Marilyn Suzanne.

Billy Joe spoke up quickly, "I'll come with you, Sybil."

"No, you're not big enough. And you've never been outside the 'Patch."

But Billy wasn't going to give up that easy. "Oh, please? I can help. Really I can. Please, Sybil?"

"Well . . . all right. But you have to promise to stay right with me and do as I say."

"Okay. I will. I promise."

They headed for the wall of kudzu. Close behind and unknown to the 'Kids followed the Stumble-Bumble BunnyBee.

Lavendar was restlessly pacing in her parlor, when in crashed the Red-Necked Buzzard, one of her helpers.

"I've found one," squawked the Buzzard. "Right out there in the middle of the field. He's only a little one, but he'll grow. There will probably be some others out looking for him before long."

Lavendar turned to Beau Weasel. "Take the wagon and bring them back. As many as you can get."

Beau Weasel started for the door. "Yes ma'am. Come on, Jack, you're supposed to be a rabbit — so hop to it."

After they left, Lavendar quietly muttered a promise to herself. "They'd better bring those 'Kids back this time, or I'll call in some more of that low-life from the swamp."

Out in the field, Sybil Sadie and Billy Joe were searching and calling for Baby Dodd. Finally they found him almost hidden beneath the branches of a blackberry bush.

"Wo," said Baby Dodd, reaching for Sybil Sadie with his chubby little blackberry-stained hands.

"Would you look at that," said Sybil Sadie. "What on earth do you think you're doing out here?"

Baby Dodd grinned, "Neatin.'"

Billy Joe looked puzzled. "Neatin'? You sure don't look neat to me!"

Sybil Sadie shook her head, "He means eating. Come on, let's go."

Just then, the Stumble-Bumble BunnyBee flew toward them and started dive-buzzing Sybil Sadie and talking in his strange buzz talk.

"Jazz-wabbizz . . . jazz-wabbizz . . . hurzzy . . . hurzzy!"

"What are you trying to tell us, Stumble?"

"Jazz-wabbizz! Jazz-wabbizz and wee-zell!"

"Oh, no! Cabbage Jack and a weasel?"

"Yezz . . . yezz!"

"Where?"

The Stumble-Bumble BunnyBee flew up and in the direction of cabbage Jack and Beau Weasel, who were quickly closing in on the 'Kids.

"Land sakes," said Sybil Sadie, "What now?"

Sybil Sadie grabbed Baby Dodd, but seeing how close Cabbage Jack and Beau Weasel were, realized there was no clear route of escape and put him back under the bush.

"You go that way, Billy Joe — back the way we came. I'll go this way to confuse them. Stumble-Bumble, you go tell the Queen. We need the BB-Bees."

They each went off as directed. Stumble-Bumble hovered for a minute, watching Cabbage Jack and Beau Weasel close in. Then he flew off toward the Castle of the Queen of the BunnyBees.

He landed with his customary bumps and rolls, almost knocking off his helmet in the process. Straightening himself up, he quickly entered a partially hidden hole in the ground. After making his way through dark passages, he burst into a hallway. Before him were double honeycomb doors, guarded by fierce-looking bees.

"Lezz me in! Lezz me in! I muzz zee the Quezz!"

The guards looked at each other and shook their heads. "Not *him* again!" said one.

Stumble-Bumble couldn't give up. "Izz emerzzy! Izz emerzzy! Jazz-wabbizz and wee-zell after 'Kizz — Cabbizz Kizz!"

The guards looked at each other again, nodded, and opened the doors to the Queen's chamber. At the far end of the room sat the Queen on her throne. Stumble-Bumble rushed toward her, tripped, and fell, and skidded to a halt at the foot of the her throne.

"Stumble! What is to be done with you? You're a threat to yourself and everyone around you each time you move. Well, I suppose your intentions are good. What brings you rushing into my chamber on a day when I was to see no one?"

"Cabbizz Kizz! Cabbizz Kizz! Emerzzy! Emerzzy!"

"Those culprits are after the 'Kids again? Sound the alarm!" exclaimed the Queen.

Immediately, a squadron of BB-Bees appeared. The Queen gave them their instructions: "Follow Stumble! The 'Kids are in trouble!"

Stumble-Bumble led the squadron of BB-Bees past the guards, down the long hall, and up into the open sky.

In the middle of the blackberry thicket, Cabbage Jack and Beau Weasel had already caught Sybil Sadie and Billy Joe. A few other 'Kids who had left the 'Patch in search of Baby Dodd were trying to help them get loose.

The BB-Bees zoomed in, in perfect formation, pelting the villains with their BBs.

Beau Weasel saw that he and Cabbage Jack were outnumbered. "Cabbage Jack, we ain't gonna get this wagon out no way! Leave it and grab what you can."

Cabbage Jack tried to grab a 'Kid, but was pelted with BBs. Finally, Beau Weasel managed to push a couple of 'Kids into a large sack and started carrying it toward Lavendar McDade's lair, leaving Cabbage Jack to face the BB-Bees.

Now, as it happened, Xavier had heard the ruckus coming from the blackberry thicket and had left Colonel Casey dozing in the sun to come and investigate the noise.

Beau Weasel saw him coming and began to run faster.

"Somebody stop him!" shouted Sybil Sadie, pointing to Beau Weasel. "He's getting away! If he makes it to those trees, won't be able to catch him!"

Xavier didn't hesitate. Remembering his favorite football strategy, he made a dash for Beau Weasel and tackled him around the knees. Beau Weasel fell, losing his grip on the sack, and the 'Kids scampered out. Seeing that the 'Kids were okay, Xavier ran back to where the BB-Bees were swarming around Cabbage Jack.

Figuring that it had worked once before, Xavier decided to try it again. He looked Cabbage Jack straight in the eye and waved his arms wildly. "Woogie-woogie!" he shouted. Now, Cabbage Jack was a bully when it came to the 'Kids, but when it came to someone his own size, he quickly gave up the fight and high-tailed it back to Lavendar McDade's.

"That was a mighty close call, Xavier," said Otis Lee. "You sure scared Cabbage Jack."

Xavier blushed at all the attention.

"It looks like you 'Kids could use some help," he said.

Then he glanced at the sky. "It's getting dark, and I've got to be home by supper."

"Oh Xavier, please don't leave," said Tyler Bo.

"Don't worry," Xavier said, "This is the best adventure I've ever had. I'll be coming back some day."

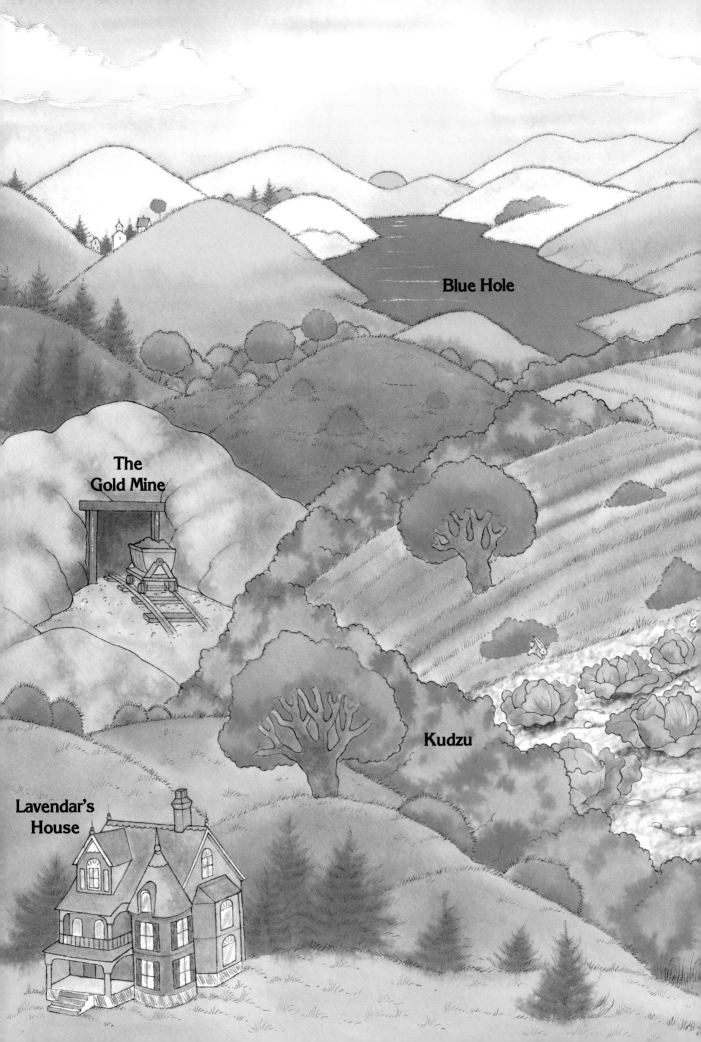

Blue Hole

The
Gold Mine

Kudzu

Lavendar's
House